CHAPTER ONE

How, in the name of all
did I end up here?

Me a teacher of classical English. A man who is well versed in Chaucer, Homer, Shakespeare, Joyce, and Pratchett, well, you must have some light relief. How on earth did I manage to end up sitting in this wire cage, waiting for somebody in uniform to come and collect me like a dog in a pound?

Nor do I have the comfort, if you could call it that, of being on my own. My cellmate appears to be a drug-dealing pimp who is dressed like a used car salesman from Hawaii. A floral shirt that does not cover his many tattoos, gold medallions and chains, and a hairstyle of slicked back dyed black hair complete with a ponytail. I am sure that he will be a big hit with the judge. He speaks with a soft Brummie accent. He was a lovely chap to talk to, but I would not want to take him home to my sainted Mother, assuming I ever get to leave this pigsty, that is.

It all began so innocently.

"Just pop down to the 'Corner Shop' and pick up some bread, will you Tom."

That was how it all started. That is all that she asked me to do. She, being Susan, my wife for over twenty-two years. A loaf of bread. Nothing more, nothing less. Simple enough. The boys will need sandwiches in their packing tomorrow for school break, and we will have our usual toast and marmalade for breakfast. I had performed this task many times before. I have had much more complicated orders to fill than just a loaf of bread, oh yes. Sometimes, I could cope with five or six items without the aid of a list, but the odds were that I would forget something and be sent back a second time to fulfil my mission. But not this time; the order was for bread, which was pure and simple.

The 'Corner Shop' was not actually on a corner at all, so the name above the door often made me smile. I think the Patel family, who opened the shop some five years earlier, had the idea that The British Corner Shop was a great institution to be retained. The fact that this shop was five shops away from the corner had little or no bearing on the name. So it became the 'Corner Shop' and appeared to be a success, being open from early morning until late at night. There was just about everything that one could need in the store and a lot that wasn't. Groceries ranged from tinned goods to fresh. Newspapers, special occasion cards, some happy and some sad, depending on the event. Toys, sweets, beer and wine, frozen items, lottery cards, etc. A proper corner shop.

It was just beginning to rain as I walked along the dirty grey pavement festooned with dark rings of discarded chewing gum looking like large raindrops, making the pathway look wetter than it was. I heard familiar voices ahead of me. Three boys wearing hooded sweaters, denim jeans, trainers, and gloves were strutting toward me.

They always looked menacing when you could not see their faces, but I knew who these boys were. They were undoubtedly trouble, but not to me. I was their English teacher from Park High School, just a few streets further towards the centre of town, and although I cannot claim that they respected me (they did not respect much these three), they never gave me too much to concern myself with.

As they approached, they were laughing and appeared overly excited about something until they saw me. Suddenly, silence was all around us. They glanced into my eyes and then down to the floor as if embarrassed about what they had been doing.

They did not stop, and I had the feeling that they would break into a run as soon as they were out of my sight. This assumption was proved correct when, as soon as they went around the corner, the sound of their running footfalls echoed off the walls of the surrounding buildings. I was sure they had been up to no good, but I was only moments away from discovering how it was to affect me.

Patel's wife and daughter ran the ‘Corner Shop’ with their father. The shop opened at 6.30 a.m. and did not close until 11.00 p.m. The ladies ran the store during the day while Mr Patel visited the various warehouses and suppliers to stock the myriad of shelves that ran the length of the shop. He would then usually rest during the afternoon until he took over for the night shift.

So it surprised me when I entered the shop not to see his brightly coloured turban sitting proudly upon his head and his cheery smile with which he greeted all his customers. What was more unnerving, however, was the disarray that met my gaze.
The countertop was almost clear of the many enticements that typically adorned its surface. All those little treats you stare at while waiting to be served and to which most of us succumb. The chocolates, the sweets, even those ridiculous small magazines with their weird headlines such as 'Aliens ate my goldfish' were no longer on the counter but instead were spread across the floor like oversized confetti from a giant's wedding.

I did not like the dread that crept over me as I called out Patel's name. There was no response. There was usually a security camera above the entrance door facing into the store, but that was among the other bits and pieces scattered about the floor.

I picked my way over the debris toward the counter and saw that the cash till was open and empty and that a large bundle of clothes was on the floor behind the counter. To my horror, I recognised the bundle to be the desperately and savagely beaten body of Patel's daughter, Rea. She had been named Rea after the Poppy, and her face was the deadly crimson shade of that very flower. Blood was on the floor and the wall; somehow, it had even found its way across the aisle to the canned food section. I just stood there momentarily, stunned, looking at Rea's poor, broken face.

I managed to shake myself free from my state of shock and went round the counter to see what, if anything, I could do for her. Just then, the bell above the door rang as another customer entered the store.

“Thank God,” I said to the man as he stepped inside and then suddenly stopped.

“Call for an ambulance and then call the Police.”

The man just looked at me as if I were mad.

“Stop wasting time”, I shouted. “Call someone.”

He snapped into action. Reaching into his pocket, he pulled out his mobile and started dialling. Thank goodness for mobiles, I thought, having left mine at home on the kitchen table.

A guttural groan of sheer anguish came from Rea’s body as I tried to raise her head from the floor. There was a sickly sound as her head was released from the sticky glutinous blood that wanted to keep her attached to the floor. Her long hair was released, and the area around me, including my clothes, was painted in a crimson spray.

I slid a handful of paper carrier bags under her head to act as a pillow and slowly lowered her back into what I hoped was a more comfortable position. The other customer leaned over the countertop to tell me the ambulance was coming. But before he got to the end of his sentence, he saw Rea's disfigured face and snapped back quickly before racing through the door and dumping his stomach contents of that evening's steak and kidney pie into the gutter to be washed away by the ever-increasing rainfall.

I suggested he remain outside underneath the awning to keep dry and prevent anybody besides the Emergency Services from entering the shop. It was just as well as the Ambulance arrived within minutes of the call. Still, after stopping at the corner shop that was actually on the corner, they were now racing to the other end of the street to the other corner when my newfound colleague waved them down to the actual 'Corner Shop.'

CHAPTER TWO

"Bastards," I thought. Those three creepy, hooded little pieces of shit. It had to be them. I did not even think about who was responsible for Rea's condition whilst I was attending to her and dealing with events. But now, in the early light of day, I had time to consider what had taken place and who may have been involved.

Of course, they had been in trouble before these three, but this was a whole new level to which they had sunk. They were involved in the recent London riots and filmed on CCTV (who isn't these days) and arrested a few days later with the electrical goods from the Dixons store still in their bedrooms.

They did not even have the guile to hide or to sell them before the police arrived and took them and their ill-gotten goods to the local nick. I still smile when I think of the defence of one of them, Taylor, it was, when the judge asked him directly if he was in the Dixons store on that dreadful night, he replied that he would not have been there because he was banned from the store for a previous conviction of shoplifting and it would have been against his probation had he entered the shop that night. I heard that even his lawyer sniggered at that defence. I cursed myself because I figured that they had done something when I saw them in the street that night, but it did not occur to me until the following day that it was more than likely that they were the thugs that had put young Rea Patel into intensive care.

The police had quizzed me for over forty minutes about what I had seen as I entered the shop and my purpose for being there. I came to understand that as the second customer walked in and saw me leaning over Rea's body, he had also reported this to the police, which made me their number one suspect. They never asked me if I saw anything of interest before I entered the shop. As I was fending off a barrage of questions relating to my purpose for being there, I simply forgot about seeing Peter Watson, Gary Miles, and their sickly little sidekick Norman Taylor coming from the direction of the shop.

Watson was the leader of the trio, there was no doubt. Whatever he said, the others would do.

Miles was the dangerous one. When Watson gave him something to do, he immediately jumped into action and carried out his friend's wishes with some relish, even adding a little extra to please his friend. Taylor was the snivelling rat. He reluctantly did what he was told because he had no backbone and hung around with the other two, mainly because he would have had nobody to talk with without them. They, in turn, tolerated him because they had the power to make him do whatever they wanted, especially as he was expendable, and if he were to be caught, they would deny him completely.

The following day, I called the police officer in charge, Sergeant Mathews and was surprised that he was still working on the case at this early hour. I told him about the three pupils of mine who I had seen on a few streets from the shop, and he promised to investigate. He did not sound convinced. In fact, he sounded angry. I got the impression that he was no longer interested in my words because he kept asking me why I had not told him about these people last night. I tried to explain, but even as I was saying it, it was beginning to sound, even to me, as if I was trying to shift responsibility.

I was tired and hungry, having skipped breakfast (no toast, obviously), and with the boys whining about fresh fruit instead of sandwiches, I decided I would head off to school a little earlier than usual. I taught English to students who thought that the letters 'th' no longer existed in the English language, having been surpassed by the letter 'f.' Students who thought that the fine actor Ray Whinstone spoke 'proper.' Where 'I fink, verfore I is' is the Kings' English. Shakespeare is rubbish, and Milton,' who's e ven'? If there is ever an occupation totally lost on the masses, then it must be teaching the classics to children who have been brought up using text/Whinstone speak.

I often complained to my colleagues at work about the poorly spoken English of the locals. They had convinced me that this is the way they speak and that it is inbred, and unless you are Rex Harrison, you cannot change them. However, I have noticed over the recent past that the black kids, sorry, coloured, or Afro Britain's, sorry again, I cannot keep up with this Political Correctness bullshit. Anyway, those kids had changed from sounding like extras in an episode of 'Eastenders' and now sounding like 'Boys from the Hood' in New York City. 'Wazup Man,' or 'Yo, waz apnin,' was their typical greeting to each other. With High Fives and wearing baseball caps back to front, they could easily be mistaken for American children on tour instead of naturalised British citizens.

I sometimes wondered if I were to turn their caps back the correct way, would they suddenly start speaking English again? I think that children can change; it is solely a case of 'only if they want to.'

As I approached the tall gates of the school, I remembered that the three deadbeats, Watson, Miles, and Taylor, would be in my first and fourth periods. I was not looking forward to this confrontation. They must know that I know. They had to believe that I would suspect them of this evil deed as it was obvious where I was going to at that time of night unless they thought I wanted a late-night Kebab or some other unsavoury delicacy.

No, this would be a difficult morning, but I was determined to persevere and not hold back on my convictions. My first visit this damp morning must be to the Headmaster's office to fill him in on the events of last night and to tell him of my suspicions and the possible repercussions for the school.

I had not reached the gates when a large group of Asian men, women, and some children swept from a side street opposite the school entrance and headed in an orderly fashion straight toward me. They were carrying banners relating to ethnic violence and racial prejudice.

I realised that this could only be about last night's attack and that I no longer needed to inform the Head about possible public reactions; he could see it quite clearly from his office window. As the marchers passed, I headed into the school grounds and across the yard with its many crisscrossing, multi-coloured sets of painted lines for various games to the main entrance under the carved shapes of two doves carrying the International sign of peace, an Olive branch. The irony was not lost on me.

The head greeted me with his usual.

"Good Morning, Perkins."

He wore his standard attire: a brown check jacket over a white shirt, a brown tie, grey trousers, and brown, highly polished shoes.

I had asked him to call me Tom for three years, but I remained Perkins.

"Did you see that dreadful display out there, and right in front of the school too. Can't they take their grievances somewhere else?"

"I think you had best sit down, Head," I said. Things could get a whole lot worse once the news gets out."

I explained to him in detail the events of last night and my subsequent call this morning to the police. His face started to turn from its normal pale, somewhat pasty colour through a range of pink to rosy and finally full-blown red.

"Do you know what this could do to this school? Do you have any idea what the school governors will say? Good God man, this could close us down."

I had not expected this reaction. I blurted out something about poor Rea, justice, conscience, and such, but I may as well have been talking to one of my fifth-form students about Chekhov. Nothing I said registered with him; he just kept whining on and on, so I pretended to listen. When the storm had passed, I excused myself and headed for the sanctuary of the staff room.

I made myself a coffee and sat in the corner of the room like a naughty little boy. I may just as well have tucked my legs under my chin, sucked my thumb, and stared at the floor. Other staff members started to enter the room, and many mentioned the march had delayed their getting to the school.

I pretended not to know anything, and they left me to stew with my coffee and my thoughts. Maybe it wasn't those three boys? Perhaps I am seeing more than there was? I asked myself repeatedly. Are you sure it was them? Unfortunately, the answer kept coming back yes. It was those three bastards. I am positive, and I am going to get to the truth one way or another.

CHAPTER THREE

The morning went relatively well. The three suspects, or at least that is what they were to me, did not show up for class.

Nothing is surprising there. Truancy was the most popular subject at Park High, and most of the students deserved an 'A' in that particular field. The lesson went well. I had asked the class to watch a portrayal of 'Henry V' on TV the previous night and to write an appraisal of 500 words. I received twelve efforts out of twenty-seven. The others all had excuses ranging from the TV being broken. 'Big Brother' was on at the same time. We do not have a television. And the best, 'I had to look after my little brother who has mumps.' I say the best because I know the girl did not have a little brother. I am well past the point of no return that most teachers reach after several years of trying their hardest to improve the education of the young.

I had expected fewer than twelve to make the effort, which was an excellent result. The rest will forge ahead into the future with the sure and solid knowledge that the state is there to support them when they leave school and that ‘work’ is something others need to do to provide the funds for their needs.

I was called into the headmaster's office at lunchtime; no surprise there either. I expected him to have thought of some more rants and raves for my ears, but I was not there to listen to him. As it turned out, I was there to be interviewed once again by the man who appears to require no sleep, Detective Sergeant Mathews. He was highly interested in my story about the three boys this time. He had sounded dismissive when I first told him, but now he seems almost keen.

I went over and over the details of the evening of the assault. A lot of attention was paid to their dress that evening. I tried to describe the hooded jackets, jeans, and gloves they wore, but to state that they were a dull, drab, nondescript colour and style would have covered most of the kids out on the street that night. Mathews then told me that he had interviewed the three children. Funny I would never describe these three as children, and they all stated that they were at their own homes that night and that they had not been near the 'Corner Shop' nor had they seen me.

"They were probably home looking after their little brothers who had mumps," I said sarcastically.

The statement was lost on the Detective, but I went on to say that they were habitual liars, and I hoped that he would not take their word over mine. I had seen them where I said, and that was a fact. He said nothing. He looked at his notes and asked me if I had ever accused the three of any offence before. I told him no, but he looked up from his notepad and asked me to think again. Once again, I stated that I had not, but then he told me that the boys were convinced that I had 'shopped them' to the Police after the riots last year.

"Most of the staff at this school were asked to view videotapes of the riots to see if we could identify anybody, not just me. And anyway, I did not pick those three out as it happened; the Head spotted them."

"That's true, Officer. It was me, not Tom, who picked them out."

"Tom, I thought, finally, after three years, he calls me Tom. Better late than never, I suppose."

"If they are blaming Tom, then they are in error."

“I see,” was all the Sergeant said before preparing to leave.

“So what are you going to do now”? I asked. “Are you going to arrest them”?

“No” came the reply. “We have no evidence, motive, clothes or gloves with blood stains, nothing, just your word.”

“Perhaps if you had told us about them on the night of the incident instead of the next morning, we could have caught them before they had time to dispose of the evidence, but you didn't. The only one there with bloodstained clothing was you”.

I hung my head again. “No, I did not, Detective Sergeant, sorry.”

With that, he left and I was again alone with the headmaster.

“So Perkins,” he said, “You seem to have gotten yourself into a right pickle, haven’t you, as well as this school and its reputation.”

“Tom did not last long, I thought. It was back to Perkins now, and I felt like the guilty party once again. Oh great,” I thought, “the day has just taken a whole new turn for the worse.”

I had entered my classroom for the afternoon session, and there to greet me were the three shits who had somehow turned my quiet little suburban lifestyle completely onto its head.

“Good afternoon, sir,” they said as one. “Sorry about this morning, but we was otherwise detained’”.

“Irony,” I thought. “I did not know that they were capable. At least something good has come out of this.” “OK,” I said, “let us move on then, shall we.”

I continued the rest of the day doing what I do and generally wasting my time as those three gits continually stared at me until, thankfully, the bell sounded to end, possibly the worst day of my three years at this school or any other school for that matter. I could finally leave their horrible looks and once again hide away in the sanctity of the Teacher's Staff room.

After brooding over yet another stewed cup of coffee, I decided that it was a police matter now and that I had best wash my hands over the whole affair. Leave it to the professionals. Let them do their jobs, and justice will prevail. I am only a school teacher, not some kind of avenging angel. Keep my head down and my nose clean, and all will be well. It may sound a little cowardly, but I am not here to investigate crime. I am here to teach and to let the authorities do their work.

I felt better now, if not entirely at ease with my conscience, as I made my way out of the school building and into the surrounding streets.

CHAPTER FOUR

"Well, stuff that idea for a start," I thought as I stood looking down at Rea's poor bloated, bruised, and disfigured face.

I had wandered through the streets heading home to my wife and children when I was suddenly standing at the Saint Joseph's Hospital entrance. When I left the school, I had no intention of walking the two miles to the Hospital, but here I was. I entered and asked at the reception where Rea was likely to be. After some security issues, I explained my relationship and was shown to her room on the fourth floor. Sitting on either side of her bed were Mr. and Mrs. Patel. Neither looked like they had slept a wink, but they still stood and greeted me as if I were a family member. They thanked me for all that I had done for their daughter, and despite my protestations, they kept thanking me and holding my hand. Mr. Patel felt responsible for being late getting back from the wholesalers and not being on duty as usual. There was nothing that I could say to ease his burden. I stood over Rea and was shocked to my boots at the look of her face. It was not a face but an over-inflated multicoloured ball with closed eyes and split lips. I felt sick to my stomach.

I was feeling anguish for Rea, shame and anger at my recent decision to have nothing to do with it, and fury at the three snivelling rats whom I knew to have done all this damage to this poor girl. How could I have even thought of letting this thing go? I wanted to punish myself, punish them, and even punish the authorities for what I did not know yet. I was so angry that I was ready to burst, but in the presence of these two dear people, I swallowed hard and asked the usual stupid questions.

“How is she”? What do the Doctors say”?

All the usual crap instead of what was really going through my mind. God, I wanted to hurt those three yobs, not like what they had done to Rea, but something much worse.

I stayed for an hour and then said my goodbyes, promising to call again soon. Rea was still unconscious, which was due to the drugs that the Doctors had administered. They said that she would be in too much pain if she were awake, so it was best to let her heal quietly whilst she remained asleep. The broken bones would heal, as would the damaged tissue, but of the mental scarring, they were unable to say. I thanked them for their care and made my way out of the hospital into the fresh air. I took several deep breaths to clear the clinical smell of the hospital room from my nostrils and calm myself down. I took out my mobile and dialled the number Detective

Sergeant Mathews gave me. I wanted to know what progress, if any, had been made. I needed encouragement of some kind. I desperately wanted to hear that they were on top of the case and that the three slugs would be arrested that very day. However, I was told that the detective was not on duty but would call me when he received my message.

“So he does sleep after all,” I thought.

I thanked the officer, but the line was already dead, so I hung up and walked towards my home.

Arriving at the gate to my house, I stopped for a moment to enjoy the normality of the situation. No more snivelling kids, no more beaten faces, just the sanctity of home.

“An Englishman’s home is truly his castle,” I thought.

I entered through the recently painted front door to be greeted with a pair of screaming, crying children and a wife in slightly more control but equally distressed and with the telltale signs of prolonged tears.

“What in God’s name has happened”? I asked.

“Come with me,” said Susan, “you boys stay here.”

We went through the hall into the kitchen and out into the garden.

“What is going on?” I asked once again.

“Look,” said Susan, pointing towards the garden shed and bursting into tears again.

“Holy Mother”, I gasped.

The shed door was covered in hair and blood. I went over to take a closer look and wished I had not. What was left of our pet cat, Othello, was nailed to the door.

"Who, what"? I could not conjugate a sentence.

"The boys found him like that when they came home from school," said Sue, "They called me straight away, and fortunately, I had left work early and was coming up the street." "Who would do such a thing, Tom"?

I was about to answer that I had no idea, but at that very moment, I had a damn good idea who it was and why.

"I can't imagine, darling," I said. "You go back and check on the boys, and I will deal with this."

With all my qualifications in English, I cannot describe what it was like taking the poor remains of my cat off that door. I can say that this had to stop before anything happened to one of my boys or my wife, Susan. I figured the cat was just a warning to keep my nose out. A lot worse would follow if I did not stop. Well, I was not going to stop. What they had done to Rea was the catalyst. This warning was supposed to frighten me off, but it had galvanised my emotions into planning for vengeance. I had never thought of myself as a cold, calculating man. Still, somehow, the events of the past few days had brought out in me an inner fury that was controlled but vicious in its manifestation, and I was going to heap pain on those boys the way they had never experienced.

CHAPTER FIVE

Another wet and miserable day had started. The boys were still weepy over the horrible death of 'Othello', and Susan had decided to keep them away from school for the day and, likewise she, away from work. On the other hand, I had slept well and was looking forward to starting a new day where I could plan for the retribution I had in mind. Walking to work was a most unusual feeling, thinking of revenge and its dreadful ramifications. I figured that, firstly, I somehow had to get the trust of Watson and his cronies, and that would not be easy. But I had a plan, and I would start after the morning break.

The lesson drifted along as usual. I speak to them in English, and they, in turn, answer in another tongue altogether. It was just as well that I was standing in front of them watching their lips move because if I had my back to them, I swear I would have had no idea what they were saying. Finally, the bell sounded, and the class stood and filed out of the door.

"Not you, Watson," I said, "I want a word with you before you go."

He stopped and looked at his two cohorts, but they continued walking. Then the door closed, and it was just him and me.

"Nice trick with the cat", I said, "very impressive. Was it supposed to frighten me or just my kids"?

"I don't know what you're talking about, Sir." He said, wearing a sickly grin.

I would have loved to have been able to punch his lights out there and then, but that was not a part of my plan.

“Doesn’t bother me either way” I said, “Stupid cat, never liked it anyway. In fact, you did me a favour.”

He looked a little bit uneasy now but still retained his smirk.

“Anyway, all this over some stupid paki girl hardly seems worth it, does it”?

My guts churned as I said those words. I was pretending to think at his level, and it was not easy.

“What’s say we call it even”?

“Still don’t know what you’re talking about, Sir. Me and the others got questioned by the cops over that stinking wog, and you put 'em on to us.”

“They questioned me as well, you know, twice. I had to tell them what I saw. I never suggested it was you three. Anyway, I doubt they will bother you anymore over it. It's not as if she is one of us, right?”

“Damn right, Sir, but it wasn’t us anyway.”

“Whatever you say, Watson, but whoever did it deserves a medal. There are too many of those wops around here. We need more action like that to show them that this is our country and that they should take their stinking ways with them and go back to whatever shithole they came from. All right, you can go.”

The classroom was now empty, but the stench of betrayal lingered like stale aftershave. I was ashamed of what I had said. Of course, I realised I did not believe a word of it, but still, having said it, I wanted to wash my mouth with carbolic soap and then swallow some to try to cleanse my soul.

Watson looked puzzled as he walked out. He stopped and looked back in my direction as if he wanted to say something whilst staring over my shoulder at the store cupboard behind me, but decided against it and continued on his way. I was a little puzzled by his look but assumed he could not look me in the eye. This was the desired effect that I wanted. I needed to get him to think that I was really on his side and that thc intervention of the Police was just a coincidence. I needed him and his two dogs to leave my family alone and consider myself a friend to their cause. I needed them out of my hair for a while to figure a way of stopping them in their tracks and getting them out of my life and the Patel's families lives for the last time.

CHAPTER SIX

The stillness of my musing was shattered when the headmaster marched into my classroom, followed by two other gentlemen with the demeanour of police officers written all over them.

"Perkins," said the Head, "these two officers wish to speak with you."

I looked at the Head and thought that he looked stressed but not unhappy with the situation.

"These officers are with the Drugs Squad."

This should have surprised me, but the Drugs Squad could have had a permanent office alongside the Matron and the Caretaker at this school, as all three were constantly on call. One officer was tall and quite smartly dressed, while the short officer looked like a rumpled pile of laundry with multiple stains on his red tie.

"Mr. Perkins," said the taller of the two officers, "we wish to look inside your desk and your locker."

Now, this time, I was surprised.

"Why do you want to do that," I asked.

The shorter officer answered my question with a frightening statement.

"We have reason to believe that there may be illegal substances that you are hiding and supplying to children within this establishment."

"No way, I replied forcefully. I do not condone drug use, nor would I ever use them myself."

"Then you won't mind if we look around," he said.

"I do not, " I replied, "go ahead."

They went to my desk, searched the drawers, and looked underneath. On finding nothing, they then asked for the keys to my books, cupboard, and private locker. As they opened the storeroom door, I suddenly remembered the look on Watson's face as he stared back in my direction. He was not avoiding my eyes as I had suspected; he was probably thinking about what he or one of his cronies had placed in my cupboard before telephoning the drug helpline with their anonymous tip for the police. He may even have wanted to warn me but had thought better of it and left before events took their course. I groaned inwardly, expecting the worst. The two officers entered the small room that acted as my store and started moving items around.

“There is a quantity of substance here that I suggest you and the Head witness before we remove them,” said the taller one.

I followed the Head into the cupboard, and sure enough, there on a shelf partly hidden by rarely used copies of

Shakespeare's Macbeth was a plastic bag containing several smaller bags, each with a small amount of white powder within. The look on the Head's face was enough to turn milk sour. It was one of pain, disgust, and disappointment.

"Needless to say, it is not mine," I said, feeling like a right berk as I said it. "How many times have they heard that," I thought.

"Please believe me, I loath drugs and would never be involved with anything to do with drugs."

"Please come with us," said the taller one, who had finally introduced himself as Officer Johnson, and away we went.

With the Head marching in front of me and the two officers in stride behind, we went outside to their car, and I was seated in the back, the taller one pressing my head down to assist my ingress as if I needed it, and I was driven away in front of the hundreds of eyes of the pupils of Park High. At any other establishment, the shame of these proceedings would have been too much for most people to bear, but at Park High, it had probably raised my 'street-cred' quite a few notches.

After being 'booked in,' which sounds like I was being registered at a Hotel, I was allowed the proverbial one telephone call and used the opportunity to call Susan.

"How do you explain the fact that you have been arrested on suspicion of supplying drugs to minors at your own school," I thought whilst the digital world used its magic to connect me with my wife.

"You have done what"? That was not the reply that I wanted to hear.

"I have done nothing, please listen to me,"

I told her what had occurred and asked her to contact our friend and local solicitor, Alan, to help me out of this mess.

“I don’t have his number, can’t you call him”? She said.

I wondered how many men had ended up arguing with their wives or partners over the telephone when they were limited to just one call and were already using up that singular privilege.

“Find it and call him, will you? I am in enough trouble here without you and me fighting.”

I regretted that statement as soon as I made it, but like many things
that husbands say to their wives when stressed, I knew that one day, it would be returned with interest, and I would not be able to defend myself.

“Has this thing with the cat got anything to do with it? Are you mixed up in some kind of drug gang thing”?

"For pity's sake, Susan, get hold of Alan, and when I get home, I will explain everything to you both."

She hung up, but I could still hear her anguish.

"How could she doubt me"? I thought. "After all these years, she should know me better than that."

I put it down to the stress of the 'Othello' incident. Mind you, she will now know I lied when I told her I did not know who would do such a thing to our pet cat. I had best tell her I thought about it later and did not want to involve the police because it may upset the boys further. But then she will rightly say that you are involved with the police, and if you had said something earlier, maybe they would suspect others and not you. I was falling upon my own sword. As Sir Walter Scott wrote, "Oh, what a tangled web we weave when first we practice to deceive."

CHAPTER SEVEN

Susan found Alan's number in the Rolodex. I keep it next to the telephone under the heading, Alan, Lawyer.

"Who would have thought to look there"? I thought, "No, I mustn't be sarcastic. I am in enough trouble as it is."

Alan arrived at the police station within the hour, having been persuaded by Susan to leave the Squash court that he was using as this was a real emergency. He was losing heavily, so abandoning the game gave him the chance of a rematch. It took another forty minutes before I was released on something called Police Bail.

"What the hell is going on, Tom," said Alan. "Susan is beside herself and threatened to drag me bodily down here if I did not get my arse into gear fast."

“I will explain when we get back home, Alan. I only want to tell this story once, so when we are all together, I will tell you everything."

I told them both the story so far, but of course, I did not mention my plans to befriend the three thugs. I thought they would not share my enthusiasm for seeking revenge for the damage that they had done to Rea. Alan told me that I had little to worry about as the drugs were not found on my person, and at least three other people had a key for that cupboard: the Head and the caretaker as well as myself. I did not share his confidence but would bow to his greater knowledge. I also apologised to Susan for losing my composure on the telephone, which I put down to fatigue. I figured that if I did it in front of Alan, I would not be hit too hard by the backlash. That idea at least seemed to work for the moment. Alan told me I was to appear the following week in front of the local

Magistrate Court. The idea of standing in front of Amateur Judges scared the pants off me, but unless I decided to commit a more severe crime, I would have to rely on them to get it right. Alan warned me that if further evidence became known, they could remand me to prison to face a Crown Court Judge in due course. This news suddenly made me appreciate the Magistrates Court much more.

As Alan was leaving the telephone rang so I answered it as Susan saw Alan to the door. It was the School Head. He asked about my welfare and tried to make some small talk, but he was not doing a particularly good job of it. I said that I would explain everything to him that afternoon when he coughed, and his voice seemed to shrink if that was medically possible. He told me that until this incident was over and my name cleared, which he was sure would be the outcome, I was officially on gardening leave. In other words, I had been suspended. I tried to plead with him, but he said that he had talked to the Board of Governors and that the decision was final.

Life was just dandy in the Perkins household. Poor Rea's battering, and then the cat. Now suspended from work and a drug charge to defend. What else could possibly go wrong? I wished I had not even had that thought as I heard Susan or felt her presence in the room. I turned to face her, and her look was like thunder.

"Susan, please, stay calm," I said.

"I am calm," she stated through clenched teeth. What I want to know is how the hell you got into this mess without telling me anything, and what's more important, what are we going to do about it? "

"What do you mean we"? I said, "This is my problem, and I will handle it."

“Oh no, you don’t. You persuaded me to leave Oxford to come to this hell hole so that you could ‘pass on your knowledge to those less fortunate’ was the way you put it to me, if I recall. Well, ‘those less fortunate’ have terrorised my children, beaten a young girl half to death, planted drugs on you, and had you taken away by the Police. That makes it our problem and not just yours. And don’t forget about the CAT.”

She was right, of course. Whatever affected me and my work also affected our family.

"And I have just been suspended from the school. That was the Head on the phone."

“Well, that's simply great. These kids do not need you to quote Keats or Chaucer; they need to be guided. For God's sake, they must be taught Basic English and Basic Maths. They are not the highbrow, privileged Oxford students you are used to dealing with; these kids are the drain diggers of tomorrow, and the world needs ditch diggers as well as academics. So come on, Tom, I know you must have a plan of some sort. After twenty-plus years, I know you inside out, and you would not just sit back and let matters run their course."

I stuttered and stammered, trying to assure her that I had no real plan, just some vague ideas. But she was having none of it and insisted that we sit down at the kitchen table over a hot cup of decent coffee and plan our strategy.

"OK, I said, here is where I am so far."

I outlined my ideas about trying to form some form of bond with the three delinquents and told her what I had done to date. I told her about the conversation with Watson and about the look he gave me before he left the room regarding the cupboard.

"I seriously think he wanted to warn me, but having given the Policc the tip-off, he probably figured it was too late."

"That's good, " said Susan, we can use that."

"How," I asked.

"Giving the Police an anonymous tip is not enough to get you charged. They will need somebody willing to give a statement that you supplied them to make the charge stand. If you talk to them again and get them to think of you as an ally, then whatever plans they had to consolidate the accusations will probably be thrown out."

"Good thinking," I said, "they would prefer to have me as a friend than an enemy if they thought it would be to their advantage. And if they are running drugs to the other kids in the school, having me in their 'gang' would be a real plus. But getting into bed with this scum really makes my skin crawl, Susan."

"I understand that, but we need to rid ourselves of these three, and this drug charge or our life here or anywhere else for that matter, will be impossible. Do you think that you will ever get another job teaching with a Police record as a drug pusher to school children on your résumé?"

"I guess not," I said. "So we need to get inside their little operation and send them away for quite a while."

We discussed ideas late into the evening. None of our plans involved the Police, as whatever we would do was likely outside the parameters of legality. Besides, the Police were hardly interested in a GBH to an Asian girl in this neighbourhood unless it led to civil unrest, and that was unlikely to happen if we kept our plans secret.

CHAPTER EIGHT

The Head of the school had agreed to allow me to clear my desk 'temporarily, of course,' he had said, but it had to be done after school hours. Well, in my book 'After School Hours', was immediately after the day's final bell had rung and the kids began pouring out of the building and across the schoolyard. I needed to be seen by Watson and Co. so that I could engage them in some form of discussion. Sure enough, the three of them were together as usual, walking towards me as I entered the gates.

"Evenin' Sir," said one of them.

I looked at them and nodded. Watson told the others to wait for him and approached me on his own.

"Sorry about the cupboard thing, Sir," he said, sounding genuine, "If I'd known you was one of us, I wouldn't have done it. Still, if nuffin' more is said then it will just go away like."

"I am facing Police prosecution, I said, how is this going to just vanish?"

"Don't worry, drugs are found all over this school every week. The cops make a fuss, grab whoever is closest, and then the Beaks dismiss the charges cus of lack of evidence."

"You seem very well informed in Police matters. Are you sure?"

"Of course I am; that's the way that they operate their business. Give the coppers something to give them brownie points, and the big stuff goes on untouched."

"You said 'they.' Don't you mean we?" Here I go again, forever the English Teacher.

"No way, I don't run this operation; this is the big league. East End gangs run this patch. I'm just the local runner."

"But what was all that with the 'Corner Shop,' I asked, feeling a little sick inside. Why beat that girl up?"

"Oh, that." "That was just a little initiation ceremony for Gary and Norman. We had been trying to get the shop to let us use it to extend our market, so to speak, but those paki's kept saying no. Finding the girl alone that night was just a bit of good luck."

"Not for her," I thought.

"Mind you, in truth, it didn't go down too well with the Boss. He told us to cool it cus paki kids were his next big target, and customers are customers, whatever their colour. He reckons that if we can't drive the bastards out of the country, then we may just as well use them to sell our stuff too until they don't know night from day."

He laughed at this, finding the thought of inflicting the agony of drugs onto Asian kids highly amusing. I looked at him in a different light. This fifteen-year-old was no better than the Hitler Youth, or worse, the guards at the camps who delighted in the torture and total humiliation of their prisoners. To coldly consider the long-term effects of what he and his cohorts were planning for a whole generation of young British Immigrants solely to make money was too much to take in. This was possibly the start of Asian ethnic cleansing right here in London.

I smiled at him and said something like, "You really are thinking ahead. I did not know you were so clever. Well done. We must speak again soon."

He left laughing at my praise whilst I headed to the school building and into the nearest toilets to release my stomach contents all over the floor.

"The caretaker is going to love me," I thought. After swilling my mouth with water, I left to remove the few items in my desk drawers.

I sat for several minutes thinking about what had been said, which made me ashamed of my race.

"Where do they get their ideas from?" I thought.

"I saw you talking to Watson at the school entrance. Do you think that is wise?"

It was the Head. He had come into the classroom whilst I was reeling from what I had heard and was now standing alongside me. I jumped at the sound of his voice.

"No, perhaps not, Head, but as I hope to be back at work very soon, it would not be prudent to ignore the children when they spoke to me, don't you think"?

"You have a point, Perkins, but as you are officially suspended, it may be to your advantage to avoid contact with any of the pupils until this nasty mess is cleared up, as I am sure it will be."

“Yes, Head, sorry, I assure you it won’t happen again.”

With that, he turned and left the room. Not an ounce of sympathy, just a job done and away to his office.

I headed home to speak with Susan. It was good to be able to share the burden with somebody else; however, I did not like putting unnecessary pressure on her shoulders.

“This thing is bigger than we thought,” I told her. I do not believe that we can handle this on our own. It is no longer just three nasty hooligans we are dealing with but apparently an East London Gang.”

I filled her in on the conversation with Watson, and she agreed with me that it was too dangerous now to proceed on our own; we needed professional help.

“Let’s call the Police Officer that you met when all this started,” she said, “Now that the stakes are much higher, he may well be more enthusiastic to help us."

I was not so sure that Detective Sergeant Mathews had the slightest interest in helping me. He seemed to dislike me immensely for some reason I was unaware of. However, he was the only Police Officer that I knew apart from the Drugs Police that arrested me, and I was certainly not in their good books, so Mathews it had to be.

I called his number, and he answered after two rings. I asked to arrange a meeting at my home, and after a couple of questions, he agreed to come around after four o'clock. That was fine with Susan and me as the boys stayed later at school for football practice.

I did what I do best. I sat and wrote the complete event from the start to today's meeting, reviewing it several times until I was sure nothing was left out. The full facts, from the 'Corner Shop' incident to Watson's conversation. I omitted mine and Susan's plans for revenge, of course, but covered those parts where I seemed to go along with Watson's ideas as the musings of an amateur detective. I knew that the real detective would blow his top at this, but I thought it was better than what he would have done if he had thought we were about to become a pair of vigilantes.

He arrived on time along with a colleague, WPC Jennings. This was a pleasant surprise. She was about twenty-eight years old with short blonde hair and a little makeup that she did not need as her small face was a delight. She smiled when she was introduced by Mathews revealing a complete set of white wrap-around teeth that lit up the room. "Not your average copper, that's for sure," I thought until I caught Susan's eye and realised that I was staring at the WPC a little longer than was prudent.

I turned my attention back to Detective Mathews, and Susan turned off her glare. I told him what had occurred and gave him my written statement of the facts. He read through my notes and handed them to WPC Jennings, who also read them. After a long silence, he looked me in the eye and said, "Don't you think you are in enough trouble as it is? You are the only suspect in the beating of a young girl, you have been arrested in possession of class A drugs and charged with dealing to school children, and now you are telling me that the East End Gangs are moving in on your territory and you want my help to remove them."

"No," I almost shouted, "It is not my territory; I do not have a territory as you put it. I do not deal drugs."

The WPC was making copious notes and was having trouble keeping up.

"I have not invited you here to help me in any way other than to rid the area of these villains who seem intent on using the young Asian community for their own profitable and violent ends."

Susan spoke for the first time. "Detective Mathews, do we look like drug dealers to you? Do you see any of the trappings of drug money around you? We both have full-time jobs, have two lovely boys, and we used to have a cat, but you know about that. We are two normal people caught up in some fictional horror novel and seem unable to escape the situation without help, which is why we called you. We do not want you to clear the way ahead for us; we want to get rid of drugs once and for all from the school, from the streets, and especially away from the children."

"OK, Mrs. Perkins," said Mathews, "I'll speak to the boys down at the station and see what we can do. In the meantime, please keep 'Inspector Clouseau' here away from those boys and from anybody else."

“Thank you, Detective,” said Susan, “I will try my best.”

With that, WPC Jennings collected her notes, and they both stood to leave.

“Remember,” said the Detective, “you have a court appearance next week, don’t be late.”

“I won’t,” I answered, showing them both to the door.

I watched them walk away down the path. I should have been ogling the walk of the WPC, but I was simply staring at their backs as they left. I was in a mental mess. What had started as a promising idea had backfired somehow, and I once again wished I had washed my hands of the whole thing.

CHAPTER NINE

I was back at the hospital to revisit Rea, this time with Susan along for support. Not to support me, you understand, for Mrs. Patel. I have always found it difficult for men to handle these types of circumstances. Man-to-man was not too bad, but man-to-woman was impossible. Susan had volunteered to be with me when I told her where I was going, and I was most grateful.

Rea was still unconscious and was to remain that way for one more day. Mr. Patel told me that she was slowly repairing herself and that the doctors were more hopeful than last week.

"Had it really only been five days since that dreadful night?" I thought.

I asked how his shop was doing since he and Mrs. Patel spent all their waking hours at Rea's bedside. He told me that his family from Birmingham had rallied around and were working the store day and night until he and his wife were able to return to some form of normality. He did not believe that day would be soon as Rea was their sole priority in life. If they were to lose her then their lives would end as well. Susan burst into tears at hearing this statement of total love and could only hold Mrs. Patel who sobbed along with her.

"I guess that you can see how I became so involved in wanting to get the people who did this thing now," I said to Susan after we had left the ward.

"I can," she said, still sobbing a little.

"Well let us hope that the Police decide to listen to us and that they take some form of action against those animals," I said as we walked back to the car.

As we crossed the Hospital parking area I could see Watson sitting on the bonnet of my car.

"Keep on walking Susan, I said to her, squeezing her hand gently, it looks as though we have company, I will meet you at the cafe on the next street."

"Are you sure?" she asked,

"Yes, please, I do not want you talking to this filth, just keep on going and I will see you shortly."

"Alright, " she said but please be careful."

"I should be ok here in such a public place. Besides, if anything happens to me I am right outside the Hospital."

Susan glared at me then squeezed my hand and left for our later rendezvous.

"Get off my car Watson," I said, deciding that being a wimp was not going to get me far.

He slid off to the ground and stood aggressively looking up at me.

"It is very empowering when you are taller than your opponent," I thought, “what do you want and why are you here?” I asked.

“I hear the police visited you at home this afternoon, what was all that about?”

“None of your business,” I replied, “now go away and do not approach me again.”

He seemed unfazed by any threats and just kept on talking in his overconfident self self-assured manner.

“The Boss wants you to store more stuff in your room, any problems?”

“Are you mad,” I said, “I am already under suspension and facing a drug charge. I am hardly in a position to help you or anybody else am I?”

“The Boss says that you don’t have any choice.”

“Tell your Boss that I do and I choose not to help you or him in any drugs business that you may have going.”

"You don't want to end up like Mr. Jennings now do you, Sir?"

The 'Sir' was stressed to become an insult.

"Jennings, what the hell does he have to do with this?"

Jennings was a former PE Teacher who had left the school under a cloud a couple of years ago and had not been heard from since.

"Remember how he pleaded his innocence about those abuse charges that were made against him until the kids involved decided for the good of the school and the community it would be best if they came forward to give evidence?"

"I remember the case, yes," I said feeling a little unsure suddenly.

"Well, it is surprising what some of the kids will do or say for a couple of free bags of powder. I heard that Jennings was living up north now on his own, his wife left him and took the kids and now he was on a register of sex offenders. Shame that eh!"

"What are you saying, Watson?" I asked

"A couple of free bags is all it takes to make charges stick, you know. Think about it, Sir." And with that, he walked away.

For a few moments, I could not move. It was a simple statement of fact. Join us and the charges go away, fight us and you will go to jail without passing go or collecting two hundred pounds. They had done it before and they were quite happy to do it again.

I gathered my wits and went off to report to Susan. I entered the cafe and was once again stunned. Susan was sitting at a table sipping coffee and merrily chatting with Miles and Taylor. She smiled as I walked over to her.

“Hello Darling, I was just chatting to these two boys from your school. They tell me that they are in your class and enjoy it very much.”

The look on her face altered when she saw my anger start to build.

“We must be going now, "
said Miles, "nice to meet you, missus,” and they walked out smiling.

“What’s wrong sweetheart, they are just boys?”

“They are not ‘just boys’ they are the dregs that we have been talking about for the past few days. Those two did the beating of Rea with their own hands whilst Watson looked on.”

“Oh my God, " she said, "I had no idea. I feel quite ill now having spoken to them.”

“It was another warning like ‘Othello.’ They are saying, "We can get to you whenever we want to.”

"Fuck Tom, what are we going to do?"

I was taken aback, I had never heard Susan use any sort of abusive language let alone swear. I realised just how frightened she must be.

"I do not have a clue at the moment Susan, I think that we should head for home and have a good think about things. I do not intend to become a drug dealer nor do I accept threats as they have just made."

So we left the cafe' and returned to the car park to collect the car and drive home.

CHAPTER TEN

“You must go to the Police,” said Alan.

“We have tried that and it hasn't got us anywhere,” I said a little too loudly.

“But Tom, these are threats against you and Sue, you can’t just ignore them,” Alan replied.

“I am not ignoring them, Alan, I shouted, I am definitely not ignoring them. I just do not know what to do. The Police think that I am mixed up in this drugs thing already and Detective Mathews is not convinced that I had nothing to do with Rea’s attack.”

“Is there anybody else that you can think of who can help with this situation,” Alan asked.

“Oh yes, I have put in a call to Columbo and Morse but they have yet to get back to me.”

"OK, Tom, sorry but if you will not go back to the real Police then there is very little that I can help you with from a legal

viewpoint."

"I know Alan, and I thank you for your help but this is one situation that only me and Susan can resolve." And with that, Alan showed himself out and we were left alone once again.

"Well Miss Marple," I said, "do you have any bright ideas because I sure as hell don't."

"None." Was all that Susan offered. No elaborations, no faint whiff or glimmer of an idea, nothing.

"Great," I thought, "I am in court tomorrow and unless I can produce some brilliant idea, or if Watson and his crew decide to change their minds I am going to be in even hotter water than I am now."

CHAPTER ELEVEN

“Due to this new evidence, this case is to be bound over to the Crown Court. The defendant will be remanded into custody until the case can be heard.”

That was it. That was all the Magistrate said, but the look he gave me spoke volumes. Apparently, three witnesses had been found and were prepared to give evidence. So here I am, sitting in this holding pen with my Hawaiian friend, about to be paraded in front of the press and whoever else decides to turn up for the show.

“So what are you in for?" my Brummie companion said with a smile. "You put the wrong wheely bin out, did you?”

I was not feeling in a humorous mood. “Same as you, I think, I said, dealing drugs to my pupils at school.”

“I would know if you were dealing in this area, " he said looking at me quizzically, "I know most the dealers around here.”

“That’s just it, I am not a dealer of any kind. It’s a long story.”

“So tell me the story, I don’t have any place to go right now, and the way that they are dealing with cases today I doubt if we will be seeing anybody soon.”

So I told him everything. Surprisingly, he just sat, listened, and seemed to take the whole sorry saga in his stride. He asked me a few questions about the Boss, which I was unable to help him with apart from telling him that they were Eastend people. He was, however, extremely interested in my theory regarding the Asian youth of the area. He asked me lots of questions about that side of the story and seemed enthralled. I hoped that I was not giving him ideas for his criminal future. He did not like to hear about the Patel family and the damage done to young Rea. The details actually seemed to unsettle him. Then when I had finished he asked me who my 'brief' was. I told him that my friend Alan was helping me but he said "Scrap your mate and use mine if you want to get out of here. I will talk to him for you and believe me, he will get this pathetic case of yours thrown out within minutes. Do as I tell you and you will be alright."

Just then the warder came and told us that we were heading back to the cells until tomorrow as the courts were running late.

"I will get my man to talk to you later. Don't worry; he will sort this out for you," said the cast member from Hawaii 5 0.

I thanked him as we were ushered back into the 'paddy wagon' I believe it is called, not that you can call them that anymore in these politically correct days, and driven back to our overnight accommodation at Her Majesty's Pleasure. This was the first piece of good news that I had had for some time and although I realised that the source of my good feelings was a drug dealer that I had only just met, any good news was most welcome even though it may be a complete waste of time.

CHAPTER TWELVE

My new drug-dealing friend was true to his word. His 'brief' was in the interview room and I was heading to meet with him. The warder opened the door to a singularly dull room with one table and two chairs. It was much bigger than the cell that I was detained in, fortunately for now on my own, so I was not unhappy with the surroundings. The 'brief' introduced himself to me as John Tattinger. He was a big man, six foot two, and well-built. Not flabby, far from it. He looked as though he could handle himself in most situations. He wore a good suit in charcoal grey and a crisp white shirt complete with a silk 'Boss' tie. His shoes were English brogues, highly polished, and looked expensive.

"So tell me the story that you told to Barry, my client," said the Lawyer.

That was the first time that I had heard the name of my ‘Hawaiian’ cellmate.

I repeated the story once again to this very astute man. He asked me lots of pertinent questions and wrote everything down on his legal pad in a fine hand. He told me that three kids had made allegations against me of supplying them with drugs. He also said that he had his team checking these kids out and that he would have news before the day was out. The ‘tip off’ to the police remained anonymous so was not of significance unless the person volunteers their name and gives evidence, which is most unlikely. The drugs being found in my cupboard were also easy to deal with. All that remained was the ‘witnesses’ and from what I had told him he suspected that he could deal with that part also.

He said that he would see me in court in the morning and that he would work through the night to put the case together.

I asked him why he or more likely Barry was helping me and all he would say was that Barry had taken a liking to me.

I was relieved that a well-established lawyer was working my case for me but I was also afraid of what I would be asked for in way of remuneration. I did not think that it would be cash, I was afraid of

what he would want. I hoped that by having him help me I was not leaping out of the proverbial frying pan and into the fire.

PART TWO

CHAPTER THIRTEEN

Darriano Izzi was a small man, 5ft 5in at best but built like a bull. His neck was as thick as my thigh and his chest was pumped up like an over-inflated tyre. He wore a suit of excellent quality but in truth, it did not sit well on his frame. His shirt and tie looked like it might be strangling him but he seemed comfortable in his attire.

He was carrying a holdall that apparently contained his overnight items: a toothbrush, shaver and aftershave, night clothes, and a change of shirt and socks. He was also standing on my doorstep and expecting to enter our home.

He introduced himself and stepped into the hallway. Darriano was not a man that you stepped in front of to bar his way. Although he was small, (you would never say that to his face), he carried himself well and his very manner demanded that you step aside.

He continued through to the living room and then politely introduced himself to Susan and the boys. He had been sent by Barry to make sure that no more ‘unpleasantness’ would occur during his stay. He explained that Barry was following up on the information that I had given to him in the detention cell below the courts last week and although he did not expect any problems he had asked Darriano to stay with the family for a short while just in case.

I was about to argue the case with him but he raised his hand anticipating my question and said that having Barry on my side was a good thing and not to be taken lightly. Susan asked how long he intended to stay to which he replied, "until Barry tells me to leave."

It was impossible to argue with Darriano, or Barry for that matter.

I faced the judge the next morning to be told that the case was dismissed due to the unreliability of the three key witnesses. None of them wanted to appear in court nor could they give coherent statements as all three were 'under the influence of drugs.' The prosecuting council had no other sustainable evidence so the case was thrown out. Amazingly Barry was sitting in the public gallery watching the whole proceedings having also been acquitted of his charges. His lawyer was doing well that morning.

So here we were, sitting with a stranger having tea and biscuits in my living room.

"So, Darriano, what is it that you do exactly?" I asked.

"I stop trouble, I start trouble, depends really." He replied.

"And what is it you are going to do for us?"

"Stop trouble I hope," he said. I must say that I was somewhat
relieved by that answer.

"Can we expect much in the way of trouble?" I was fearing the worst.

"Probably not once they know that I am here," he said reassuringly.

"Good, I said breathing a little slower, yes that's good news isn't it kids?"

The boys were just staring at Darriano not saying a word.

"Have you done this type of work before I heard myself asking?"

"It is not something that I do often," he said "I don't normally stay in other people's homes, I generally just visit people and that is usually enough."

"Oh" Was all I could say. "Well we can make a bed up for you and see that you have everything that you need for your stay," I said, as if he were a long-lost visiting relative.

"Don't bother" he replied, "I will stay on the couch through the night and be gone each day before breakfast. I won't be sleeping. If Barry wants me here on weekends I will let you know."

"Great" was all that I could mutter. "Sounds fine eh kids?" Still, they sat and stared as did Susan. "Well we will be going up now won't we kids so you just make yourself at home and we will see you tomorrow sometime. Goodnight."

Darriano just nodded and sat back staring ahead.

As soon as we got upstairs Susan started to fire questions at me through clenched teeth and muted despair. "What the hell is going on?" Who is this guy, he looks like a bouncer cum thug?" "Why is he staying in our house without even asking?" "Why did you let him in?"

I tried to keep calm by saying that I did not let him in, he just came in. He is staying in our house because he has been told to by Barry and I do not think that he would go on our say-so. It appears that he just does as he is told by Barry and nobody else. "You are welcome to try to eject him if you want to," I added. "Oh no you don't," she said pointing a long finger at my chest, "you let him in so if anybody is going to get rid of him then it's you."

Great, I thought, threats from school kids, threats from the police, a man that looks like he has come straight from a Don Corleone movie in my living room, and now my wife is giving me a tough time. I cannot wait to see what tomorrow has in store.

As it turned out I did not even have to wait until morning.

CHAPTER FOURTEEN

"Tom, Tom wake up!" "What is it?" I said feeling very drowsy, "what's going on?" "Listen, can't you hear it?" I listened to the sounds of the night. A dog barked in the distance, a car door was shut in a neighbouring street as a late-night reveler or a shift worker arrived home, then I heard what had awoken Susan. It sounded like somebody sitting on a bean bag or stuffing plastic bags of rubbish into bins. The sound of air escaping or, just maybe somebody being punched in the stomach several times, or several people being punched several times. I got out of bed to look out of the window. There was no light from the street able to reach the rear garden and as it was a cloudy night there was hardly any chance of seeing what was happening. But there was definitely something going on right below our bedroom window. I decided that it was probably best not to stick my head out and look down, instead, I would tell our guardian angel, Darriano, as this was much more in his line of work than in mine. I took the stairs two at a time and went into the living room just as Darriano was entering through the rear door. "What was going on out there?" "It's OK Mr. Perkins," said Darriano, "just a little altercation with a few of your students. As I said, once they know that I am here there shouldn't be any problems. They now know that I am here. Go back to bed, it will be quiet from now on."

I went back up and told Susan and we both got back into bed and stared at the ceiling, hardly getting a wink of sleep through the rest of that long night.

The next morning Darriano was gone, however, sitting on the couch was Barry looking like an extra from a desert island film. Outside his black

Range Rover was parked in the driveway with its gold wheels and black tinted windows looking every bit like a pimpmobile. “Nice car,” I said. “Oh that, don’t worry about that, said Barry, I use it to impress the punks that work for me. They love that sort of stuff. Same with the shirts and the bling, they love it. Personally, I hate this stuff. At home, my car is an old Aston Martin in silver with red trimmings and as for me I prefer jeans and polo shirts to this flowery crap, but what the heck, the punters love it and business is business.”

“So tell me, Barry, what is it that you want from me? Not that I don’t appreciate you getting me out of that scrape with the police but we do not have much money and we most certainly are not going to become part of your ‘business’ so why are you here and why the protection.”

“OK, I will tell you. What you don’t know about me is that my main activities take place in the Midlands. I pretty much control the whole of central Britain, but I can only do that with the cooperation of the Asian community. I ply my trade with everybody bar the young Asian groups. In fact, part of my 'arrangement' is that I protect them when I see outsiders trying to ease into their areas and I see to it that they don't bother them again. Now I am not saying that they are all pure and free of vices but I do not deal with them and nor do any other outsiders. So when you told me your little story about those punks who were trying to almost eradicate the Asian families with their drugs I reported back to the Elders that I deal with and they asked me to help them to sort out the problem down here. I can tell you that it is a much bigger job than you can possibly imagine. The local Elders here used to have the same deal, but they have lost the plot and are being run off when they protest because the deal here seems more racially motivated than just ‘business’ if you know what I mean. They are supplying the Asian youth with tainted goods and drugs that will get them hooked within weeks and then they will turn up the heat and supply stuff that will permanently damage the user. I am talking about brain damage, kidney failure, and ultimately death.”

“But isn’t that exactly what you are doing by supplying drugs to kids,” I said feeling a rush of bravery that my legs didn’t recognise so I had to sit down.

“No, not at all. What good is a dead customer? Supply and demand requires an end user and if that person wants and can buy the stuff then the business carries on. The TV only ever shows drug dens, down-and-outs, junkies, and the like. Most users are not like that at all. What seems to be happening down here is a culling of one group at a profit and when they are all gone it will be back to business as usual but without a large group of the local Pakistanis and Indian youth. Look, I know that I am no saint and that you probably hate me and all that I represent but I am their only hope. The police won’t do anything because they must act within their own rules, but me, I don't.

“And what about the altercation outside our house last night”? “What about the three yobs that I am dealing with”?

“Gone”, was the reply.

“When you say ‘gone’ what exactly do you mean”?

“Just gone Tom, let’s leave it at that”.

“I am trying to formulate a plan to sort this mess out but I may need your help with a few minor details, nothing much, just keeping me informed of any other incidents”.

You have my number, call me when you have decided what to do but don’t leave it too long”. And with that, he let himself out and drove away.

Susan had been standing next to me without saying a word. She looked at me with her mouth open but nothing was coming out. “Sit down and I’ll make us some tea,” I said and headed to the kitchen. When I came back she was sitting but still with the same open-mouthed expression on her face. Eventually, she spoke. “You mean to say that there were people outside our house intending to do us some serious harm last night?” “That’s what it sounds like but Darriano seems to have dealt with it.”

“I know he dealt with it, that is my point, " she shouted, but how did he deal with it? Did he threaten them, did he beat them, or worse, did he kill them?”

“I doubt it was too bad, I said with little belief, they are only kids after all.”

"Kids, Kids," shouted Susan. "We have kids, our two boys are kids, these monsters are drug dealers, thugs, animal killers, and sadists. They are not kids, they are scum and if Darriano and Barry have got rid of them then that is not such a terrible thing. The terrible thing is who will come in their stead?"

CHAPTER FIFTEEN

I called Barry that evening and told him that we would help if we could but we were not prepared to be accessories to murder or anything of that ilk.

He seemed quite taken aback. "What the hell do you mean? I took care of those three boys but that does not mean that I killed them for god's sake, what kind of a man do you think I am? They are simply now working for me under strict supervision in the Midlands where they cannot bother you again."

My relief was overpowering. All night Susan and I had been worrying about the consequences of telling Barry about my problems and what his resolution had been. At least now I could tell Susan that all was well and that the three thugs were out of our hair for good without us having been complicit in their demise. At least that was what I was going to tell her. I was not so sure. I remember my Father telling me when I was young that my slightly aggressive dog had been sent away to 'live on a farm' where it would have lots of room to run around and play with other dogs and be incredibly happy.

I did not think that Watson, Miles, and Taylor were going to be playing on any farm.

I reported back to Susan about the thugs and the relief on her face said everything. I had been so engrossed in my own situation that I had failed to notice what effect it was having on my wife. Her face lit up with the knowledge that she could sleep again at night without the thoughts that kept her awake for so long. She started to cry. I hugged her and she held me tight. "I'm sorry, I said, we will get through this one way or the other. I doubt if Darriano will be here tonight so a glass of wine and an early night are in order." She looked up at me in a way that had been missing from our relationship for some time and she said, "Forget the wine, let's go upstairs right now."

CHAPTER SIXTEEN

I have been back at work now for two weeks. After the disappearance of Watson and company, the Headmaster had called me to his office and after a lengthy lecture told me that I was to be reinstated forthwith and to commence work the following day. "Just as well that there is a shortage of teachers in this area," I thought. With Watson having suddenly left the area with his fellow cohorts there were to be no more visits from the police or trouble with anybody else, or so I had imagined.

Rea was out of the hospital and was in the loving care of her parents above the 'Corner Shop'. She was mending quickly but I doubted if she would ever work on her own again in the store below.

Susan and I had visited her twice since her release from the care unit and she was looking much better although she still had little recollection of the events of that awful night. I have heard that the memory does come back eventually if not a little slowly. I hoped for Rea's sake that those dark memories would stay hidden for an exceptionally long time.

"Mr. Perkins?" The question was obviously addressed to me because that is my name, but who is this man? I was just leaving the school grounds when the gentleman addressed me. "Yes," I said, "How can I help you?"

"I am looking for some of your pupils who appear to have left the area quite suddenly."

At first, I thought that he was from the police but the quality of his suit was not in the pay grade of the local force. Nor had he shown me any identification. No, this man was not an officer of the law, or any other legal body.

"They are not my pupils but pupils of the school and the local education authority" I stated.

"Don't be pedantic Mr. Perkins, you know exactly what I mean and to whom I refer".

"He is definitely not a former pupil of this school," I thought. "I assume that you are referring to Watson," I said.

"That's right, Watson and his two friends. The last time I spoke to them they were going to pay you a visit to your home and since then I have not heard a word from them. Do you know where they are Mr. Perkins?"

"I'm afraid I cannot help you Mr. er, you never introduced yourself," I said rather weakly.

"No, I didn't did I. Let's just say that Watson and the others are personal friends of mine and if anything untoward has befallen them I would be very angry."

He stepped up very close to me and I went weak in the knees. I could smell his breath which was not unpleasant but far too hot.

"So, where are they?”

"I, I, I don't know where they are" I stammered. I was now in fear and started to sweat a little too much. I hated to think about what was going to happen next.

"I only start back tomorrow myself so I have had no contact with Watson for some weeks."

"Not good enough, I want to know where they are," he said.

“I really dont know where they are” I said, but this did not stop the man leaning in even closer.

"Everything all right Tom," a disembodied voice said from behind me. "Can I help in any way?"

It was Darriano, like an angel appearing from Heaven, if angels look like prize fighters. Darriano stepped between me and the suit, and immediately, the suit stepped backwards. Darriano has that effect on people.

"No, this gentleman was just asking about someone from the school but I told him that I could not help him."

"Then we should be on our way then, your wife is cooking something special for us this evening and we had best not be late. Nice to meet you Mr. ?"

The suit turned on his well-dressed heels and strode away angrily to a waiting Mercedes.

CHAPTER SEVENTEEN

"What the hell was that all about?" I asked Darriano. "Who was that man and how does he know about Watson and co?"

"I can only tell you that he is a local Eastender trading in this area, as for the rest you will need to talk to Barry. I will call him now and set up a meeting."

"And another thing," I said, "not wanting to sound ungrateful but where the hell did you suddenly spring from"?

"I told you, I am here to ensure that nothing untoward happens to you or your family, so I am never too far away that I cannot assist if needed."

"Bloody hell, I thought, please don't tell me that I am about to get in the middle of a drug turf war, Susan will kill me even if the drug dealers don't."

We walked back to my car and drove the rest of the way home in silence.

On arrival, I asked Darriano not to mention the dealer to Susan and he agreed. He does not talk much anyway so keeping silent, for him was not a hardship.

As I entered the house Susan greeted me with a smile but that soon disappeared when she saw Darriano.

"Look who I bumped into outside school, I said, so I invited him back for some supper. Hope that's alright."

"Of course it's alright. Supper will be ready in fifteen minutes and then you can tell me the truth about 'bumping' into Darriano".

Susan was no fool and in fact, I was the fool thinking that she would not realise instantly that something had happened to bring Darriano and me once again to be sitting together in our dining room.

Over supper, I told her what had happened and she was a little upset, to say the least.

The recent past had taken its toll and the thought of the Big guys getting involved was just too much.

"Are we talking gangsters here? people with guns? Mobsters? Drug barons, who can make us disappear?”

Susan does watch a lot of TV so her imagination was having a field day.

"Please Susan, let’s wait until Barry gets here and listen to what he has to say."

"Barry! Isn't Barry the one who made those three bastards vanish? Isn't he the one who has brought this latest calamity onto our shoulders, Barry, what the hell is Barry going to do?”

"Susan, I almost shouted, Barry, did not beat poor Rea to a pulp. Barry did not put drugs into my school, Barry did not plant drugs in my store cupboard, or call the police and had me arrested. To date, Barry has got me out of jail and the case dropped, removed the daily threat from Watson and his gang, and stopped a dangerous incident from happening to me outside the school today so, although you know that I cannot condone how he makes a living, he is far from the cause of our problems, he has been the only thing between us and God knows what."

"Thanks for defending me," said Barry. He had walked into the house through the rear door and was standing at the entrance to the living room listening to our discussion. He was unrecognisable from the bling-bedecked, loud-shirted hulk that had last visited our home. This time he wore a superbly cut suit, Armani if I were to guess, a brilliantly crisp white shirt, blue striped tie, and Gucci loafers. It suited him perfectly. Had he told me he was a barrister I would have believed him.

"I understand your comments Mrs. Perkins but quite honestly your problems were far greater before I met your husband. I realise
how stressful this can be but you and your family will not be harmed in any way, I can assure you of that. Perhaps we could have some tea and then discuss how we can resolve this issue for the last time."

CHAPTER EIGHTEEN

"Firstly, we know who is behind the drugs going into your school. We know their names and where they are based. We also know that the attack on the girl in the shop was not a part of their plan, that was Watson's idea trying to ingratiate himself with the higher echelons of the organisation. The planting of the drugs was once again Watson's idea."

I must confess, I thought, perhaps I did not give Watson enough credit, he seemed to be thinking for himself quite a lot.

"How do you know all this," demanded Susan.

"Watson 'volunteered' the information to me," said Barry coyishly.

"Oh," said Susan. Nobody wanted to pursue that line of questioning any further.

"Watson had become a bit of a problem to his superiors and your encounter this morning with Matt Pearson, the 'handler' of Watson, was not so much a threat against you for not going along with Watson's plan to distribute drugs in the school, it was more a need to find out where Watson and his cohorts were hiding out. His superiors wanted to 'discuss' things so they now assume that he and his mates have done a runner. They do not know where to look so they wondered if he had been back in touch with you and perhaps you had some idea of where they were."

"But apart from what you have told me I don't know where they are."

"I realise that Tom but they don't know that. Besides, their 'disappearance' will blow over very soon. You don't want them around, the dealers here don't care if they stay away because if they were to turn up they would be facing some heavy problems, and all in all they are better off where they are."

Again, nobody asked the obvious question.

"So we are left with the problem of the Asian community. How to handle this particular threat," said Barry. "We cannot involve the police because they will want to interview Watson, we can't expect to appeal to the better side of the dealers because they don't have one and we don't want to get into a dealer war as this can affect people in my area as well as down here. God, I hate London."

"Any ideas?”

We all just sat there with blank expressions on our faces and stared at each other.

Suddenly Susan smiled for the first time since I arrived home that day. "I recently worked part-time for the census group compiling race and ethnicity numbers in various parts of the South including London. If I remember correctly 18% of Londoners were of Asian, mixed, or other ethnic groups. That means that approximately one and a half million people in London are under the control of the elders. You told us Barry that in the Midlands the Asian elders are in control and you work with them is that correct?"

"Yes," said Barry, "But down here the elders are not as controlling as they are in the Midlands."

"But what if the Elders from your area were to meet with the elders from London, surely they can persuade them to meet these 'dealers' head-on, and with the backing of one and a half million people behind them I am sure that anybody with a sense of self-preservation will realise that to continue with a profitable business such as theirs it would be in their best interest to forget about 'ethnic cleansing' and to concentrate on their filthy but lucrative business. No offense Barry."

"None taken," Barry replied. "It makes sense. I will travel back tonight and meet the relevant groups tomorrow. In the meantime Susan here is your back door key, don't leave it open, any undesirable could walk in."

He smiled and Susan blushed. Then he and Darriano left leaving Susan and me to consider what had taken place and to hopefully put our lives back together finally. It had only been a matter of a couple of months but that was enough for me for a lifetime.

CHAPTER NINETEEN

There was to be no meeting between the Elders in London and the dealers, they were simply too afraid and did not believe that they would be listened to anyway. Barry had been up and down the M40 between the two groups so many times that Henry Kissinger would have found it exhausting. There was no way that the Elders would expose themselves to the dangers so the Midlands elders then took it upon themselves to try to sort the problem directly with the dealers. That had not gone well at all. Two were hospitalised and the others in the delegation were threatened and warned that if they showed their 'paki' faces in the area again then they would not be leaving in one piece.

"So what next Barry," I asked as we sat having coffee in a local Starbucks. "If they can't handle it what are the options, if any?"

"Well, I don't like it but the people in my area have an idea and it is pretty radical, to say the least."

"Go on," I said,

"You won't like it Tom," he said. "OK here goes."

He outlined the plan and I must admit that it sounded like a script from a Die Hard movie.

"The elders want to contact certain people back in India and fly them out to 'resolve' the situation," he said. What that involved was not a subject that we discussed, the implied message was enough.

"Bloody Hell Barry, this is getting completely out of hand."

"I know, but what they are planning down here is pretty horrific too don't you think?"

“Well, yes, of course, but Barry, this will get very messy.”

“Honestly, I do not think so. It will have repercussions of course but not for you or me but it might backfire on the Asian community if news gets out.”

“Gets out,” I almost shouted, “how can it not get out for God's sake?”

“Listen, people come and go a lot in this ‘business.’ This is the only group that seems racially motivated, all the others are only interested in making money and keeping their heads down, so I doubt if they will be missed. The elders from the Midlands are willing to meet with the other dealer groups once this is sorted and to put their case.”

“Well good luck with that,” I said, and I meant it. “Radical problems do sometimes require radical solutions, but God, this is way beyond me.”

“Anyway, you will hear soon enough, I would imagine,” he said, “I am only telling you this in case you or Susan hear things and put two and two together and ask the police if this is connected. If you do that, we are all in trouble”. I told him that I would speak to Susan and that we would keep everything private. And we left it at that.

It was only five days later that Susan and I were sitting watching the local news on TV when the Headline, “War breaks out between drug gangs in London,” appeared on our screen.

According to the media, several people had been killed in an apparent drug-related crime, four men between the ages of twenty-eight and forty-five who were known to the police were dead from a single bullet wound to the head. Mafia style is how they described it. ‘Police have no current leads but are appealing for witnesses.’

Susan stared at me and I at her. “Good grief, is this what I think it is?” she asked.

“I guess so,” I said, “I don’t really know what to think.”

She started to cry and I felt pretty helpless as I put my arm around her shoulders.

“Hopefully, this is the end of this nightmare,” I said, not believing that to be true.

“I certainly hope so,” Susan said between sniffles, “I can’t handle this lifestyle any longer Tom.”

I just held her close and said a private prayer to the Gods to make our situation better.

CHAPTER TWENTY

So, here I was once again walking to the corner shop. I had decided to get a bottle of wine and a box of chocolates so that Susan and I could binge-watch a tv series and try to forget about recent events.

It was dry for a change, but the area still looked tatty and unwelcoming. There was no need to worry about anything nasty on this trip, though. Wrong again. When will I learn?

I had not walked along these streets since the terrible incident which started this whole episode. I actually felt nervous for some reason but there should be no cause for alarm. The problems were all behind us now, but I could not help glancing back over my shoulder every now and again. I thought that I could hear footsteps but I put it down to an overactive imagination. Wrong again.

Suddenly from out of the shadows behind me came a very scruffy and disheveled man wielding a large knife. "Shit," I thought, "this is it". "Who ARE you", he yelled into my face. He looked panicked with wild eyes and a very stressed face. "We don't know anything about you other than as a stupid school teacher, who the hell ARE you"? He was yelling into my face so close that his spittle was spraying onto me and the knife was now held just below my chin.
He screamed into my face again with the same question. The blade punctured my skin and I could feel a little blood dripping down my front. I suddenly recognized him as Matt Pearson, the suave and sophisticated Mercedes-Benz driver who had confronted me at the school gates. He was certainly not calm or sauve today and I thought that my time

here was about to come to a very messy end. As he looked into my eyes with his mad stare I thought that it was over.

Suddenly his eyes took on a puzzled look as though he could not quite understand something. Then his head turned sharply to the right with a crack that echoed off the walls. He slowly slid to the ground in front of me and I was left staring at his limp body at the feet of Darriano. "Come on, let's move," he said as I gaped at the corpse in front of me. "Come on, we do not want to stay around here any longer". He led me away, down the side streets, and escorted me back to my front door. I let myself in and fortunately, Susan had gone upstairs and was running a bath. I sank onto the sofa, put my face in my hands, and allowed the moment to flow over me. I could not tell Susan about tonight under any circumstances. I know that we agreed 'no secrets' but this was too much. I shouted upstairs that I had forgotten my wallet and I was off again to the supermarket this time in the car as they have a better choice of wines. I drove to the shopping precinct and parked well away from the store in a distant corner of the large car park, just trying to compose myself.

Fortunately, the knife had only nicked my skin, and a bit of tissue paper and spittle seemed to have staunched the flow. I sat in the car for several minutes trying to get my thoughts back together. The silence was everywhere.

"Shit", I shouted. The knock on my window nearly making me release my bowels. "For fucks sake Darriano, I nearly died when you knocked on the glass". "Twice in one night", he said, "now that's impressive. Are you ok"? "Yes, I'm just trying to gather my thoughts. Thank you for what you did for me, I was just frozen looking at that knife". "No worries," said Darriano, "He was the only one who was out of town when the main group was dealt with. I was watching you when I spotted him walking behind you. I must admit that I didn't expect him to try anything but he was obviously highly agitated. Oh well, he was the last of them so have a good evening, and please, don't get into any more trouble. Goodnight".

He actually smiled for the first time since I had met him. Now there is a man who enjoys his work.

CHAPTER TWENTYONE

Apparently, there are Gods after all, and not just Vidar, the god of vengeance, who answered my prayers last night with Darriano.

Their messenger came in the form of Barry who appeared on our rear doorstep once again, he never seemed to like using the front entrance.

“May I come inside?” he asked as if we could say no.

“I thought that I would call round and let you know what has happened over the last four weeks. Firstly the ‘problem’ was sorted and the Elders visited the other dealers to explain why action had needed to be taken. Not surprisingly none of the other dealers objected. Furthermore, I have taken over this area as well. Some didn’t like the idea but the Elders persuaded them that it was in the interests of the Asian community that someone that they trusted was in charge here. So, there you have it, now I am working in Bloody London but better me than some of the other scumbags, begging your pardon Susan."

"So no more worrying nights, no more fear of noises, and no more threats?" I said.

"Not unless you have done something else that you haven't told me about Tom?" said Barry with a smile. "I think that most of the loose ends have been tidied away too", he said looking straight into my soul.
Fortunately, Susan did not seem to notice.

"Anyway, I must go. There is lots to do. I probably won't see you again, so have a good time and don't work too hard. Oh, I almost forgot. I have a letter from Alan D Sunderland, Professor of

English Literature at Oxford University, offering you a position there. He says if you can contact him soon for a chat, then the job is yours."

Susan's face lit up.

"But how." I stammered, "How on earth did you wangle this Barry?"

He smiled broadly and said, "Not all my clients are the dross of this world as most people think, the majority are responsible, respectable people, also they are the ones that can afford quality products. Take care of yourselves".

And with that he left, leaving Susan and Me staring at the letter.

"I don't know what to say." was all that I could mutter to Susan. "What do you think?"

"I think that you get on the telephone right now, take the job, we pack the house up and get the hell out of here as soon as possible. You have done your bit and it nearly broke us, so let's get out of here and start living the life that we promised each other and that we promised to the boys."

And so I did.

Printed in Great Britain
by Amazon

48941333R00073